Micawber

JOHN LITHGOW

ILLUSTRATED BY
C. F. Payne

ALADDIN PAPERBACKS
New York   London   Toronto   Sydney

To David, Robin, and Sarah Jane
—J. L.

To all the Rockwells and Wyeths, for the
inspirations they forever offer
—C. F. P.

ALADDIN PAPERBACKS
An imprint of Simon & Schuster Children's Publishing Division
1230 Avenue of the Americas, New York, NY 10020

Text copyright © 2002 by John Lithgow
Illustrations copyright © 2002 by C. F. Payne
ALADDIN PAPERBACKS and logo, and colophon are
trademarks of Simon & Schuster, Inc.
Also available in a Simon & Schuster Books for Young Readers
hardcover edition.

Designed by Paula Winicur
The text of this book was set in Esprit.
The illustrations for this book were rendered in mixed media.
Manufactured in China
First Aladdin Paperbacks edition October 2005
10 9 8 7 6 5

The Library of Congress has cataloged the hardcover edition as follows:
Lithgow, John, 1945-
Micawber / by John Lithgow ; illustrated by C. F. Payne
p. cm.
Summary: Micawber, a squirrel fascinated by art, leaves a museum with an
art student and secretly uses her supplies to make his own paintings.
ISBN 978-0-689-83341-0 (hc.)
[1. Artist—Fiction. 2. Museums—Fiction. 3. Squirrels—Fiction. 4. Stories in
rhyme.] I. Payne, C. F., ill. II. Title.

PZ8.3.L6375 Mi 2001
[Fic]—dc21
2001020919
ISBN-13: 978-0-689-83542-1 (pbk.)
ISBN-10: 0-689-83542-6 (pbk.)
0214 SCP

One Sunday in springtime, Micawber arose
From his Central Park Carousel nest.
He straightened his whiskers and polished his nose
And set off for the place he loved best.

He scampered past
pigeons and poodles
and geese,
Past boathouse and
band shell and zoo,
Past joggers and
skaters and mounted police
To a palace on Fifth Avenue.

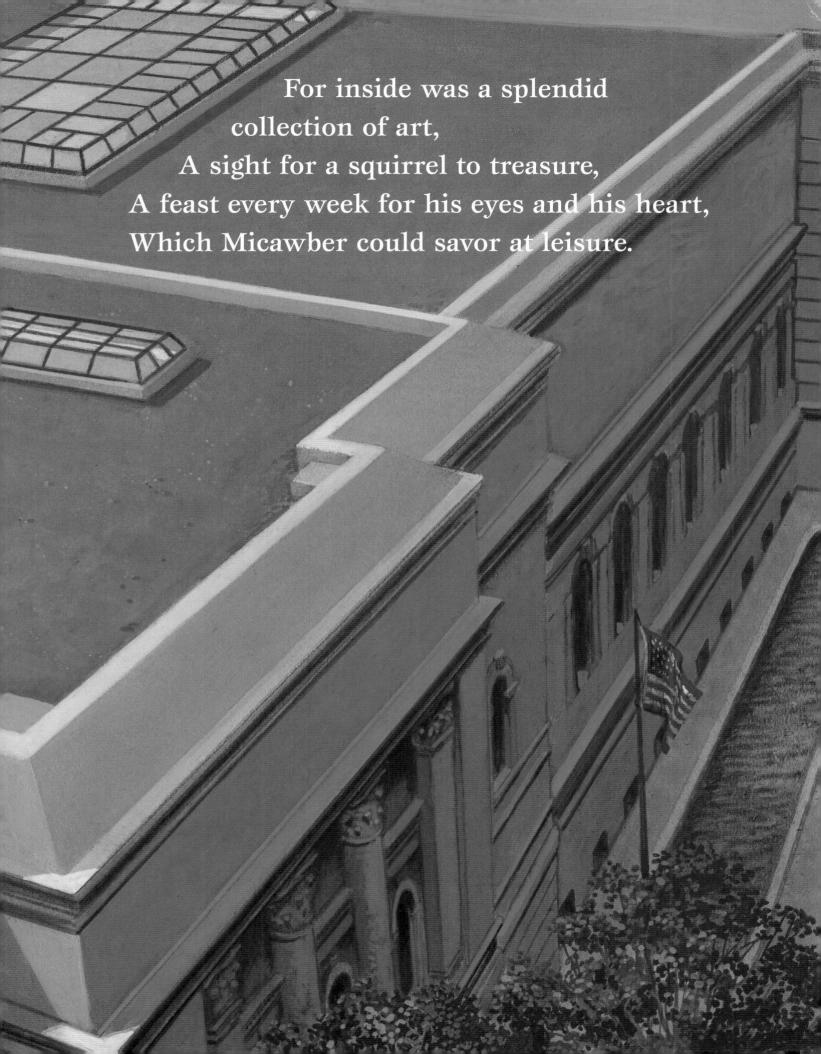

For inside was a splendid
collection of art,
A sight for a squirrel to treasure,
A feast every week for his eyes and his heart,
Which Micawber could savor at leisure.

Through the windows he'd gaze at Van Dyck
  and van Gogh,
Appraise every Rembrandt and Titian.
He would scrutinize Rubens, peruse each Rousseau,
Inspect each Lautrec and Cassatt and Miró.
He would find a new favorite each time he
  would go,
And nobody charged him admission.

But a stranger appeared this particular day
As Micawber peered down through a skylight.
She stood at an easel beneath a Monet
That depicted a haystack at twilight.

Micawber observed her for hours on end
As she copied each texture and shade.
He noted the stroke of each brush she'd extend,
The rare concentration and care she'd expend.
She'd become his unwitting and unknowing friend
By the time the day started to fade.

So he hid in the box where her paints were all
   stowed
While she bicycled home unawares.
Then he sneaked himself into her modest abode
As she hauled her equipment upstairs.

From the box after midnight the stowaway crept,
Stretched his limbs and adjusted his eyes.
And while his beguiler contentedly slept,
He rifled through all her supplies.

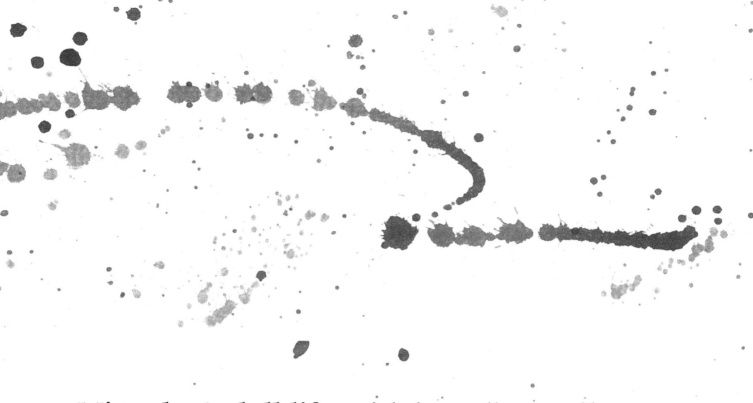

Micawber's dull life, with its tedious toils,
All at once seemed a hundred times duller,
As he straddled a palette and squeezed out
  some oils
And discovered the wonders of COLOR!

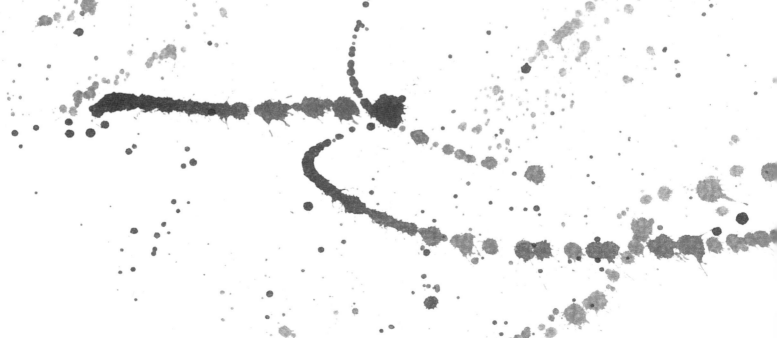

He daubed at a canvas with cadmium green,
Employing his tail as a brush.
Then magenta, vermilion, ultramarine,
Alizarin crimson, and bright tangerine;
Such a radiant rainbow he never had seen—
So splashy and lavish and lush!

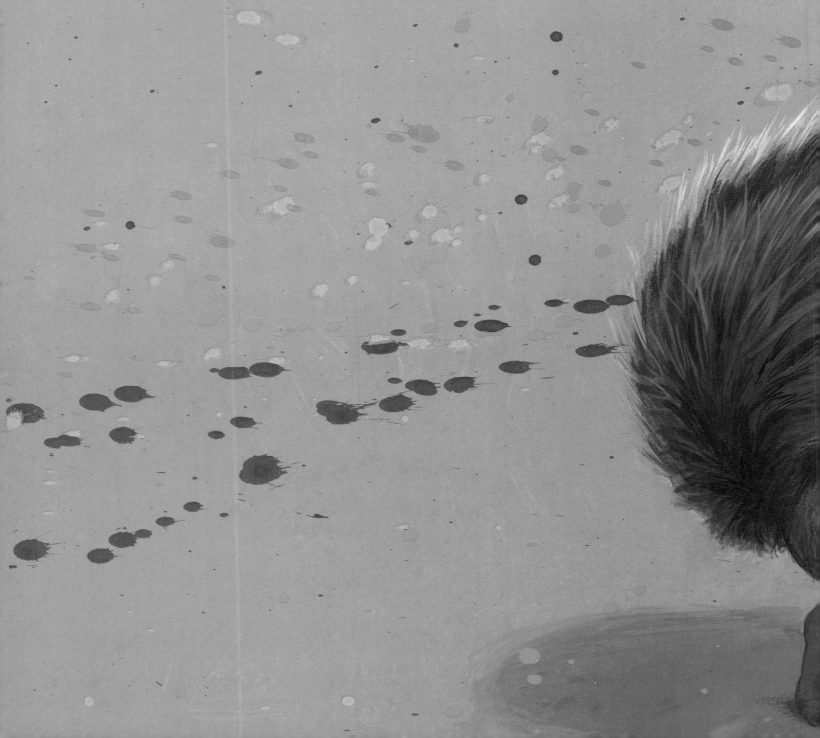

By morning Micawber was finally done
And so proud that he practically fainted.
He'd been looking at paintings from day
  number one,
But never a painting he'd painted.

As the sunlight poured in, he was ready to go,
Leaving everything just as he'd found it.
Through the transom he scrambled, his canvas
  in tow,
Rolled up with a shoelace tied round it.

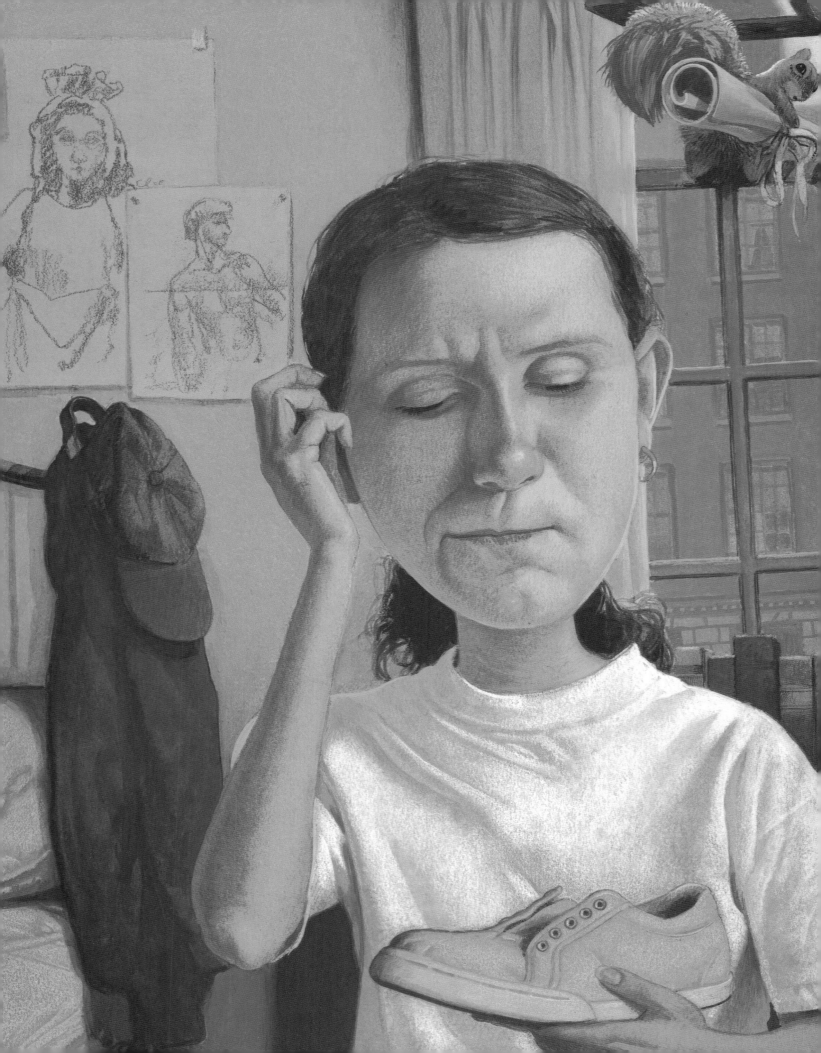

A truck trundled by as Micawber alit;
On the side it said, PARK SANITATION.
He bounded aboard it, ignoring the grit,
And completed his peregrination.

He returned thirty times by the following fall,
And the paintings poured forth like a geyser.
He fastened them all to his living-room wall,
And the woman was never the wiser.

So if some July you should chance to pass by
A viridian Central Park dale,
Look around for a squirrel with a gleam in his eye
And some paint on the tip of his tail.

And if you should visit the old Carousel,
Look up at its uppermost part.
Inside, although nobody ever could tell,
A talented squirrel continues to dwell.
If you try, you can picture it, clear as a bell: